The Bandit

Dave and Pat Sargent are longtime residents of Prairie Grove, Arkansas. Dave, a fourth-generation dairy farmer, began writing in early December of 1990, and Pat, a former teacher, began writing in the fourth grade. They enjoy the outdoors and have a real love for animals.

The Bandit

Animal Pride Series
Book 14

By

Dave and Pat Sargent

Beyond The End
By
Sue Rogers

Illustrated by
Jeane Lirley Huff

Ozark Publishing, Inc.
P.O. Box 228
Prairie Grove, AR 72753

Cataloging-in-publication data

Sargent, Dave, 1941-
    The Bandit / by Dave and Pat Sargent ; illustrated by
Jeane Lirley Huff. —Prairie Grove, AR : Ozark
Publishing, ©2003.
    ix, 36 p. : col. ill. ; 21 cm. (Animal pride series ; 14)
    "I help others"—Cover.
    SUMMARY: When a young weasel family loses
their mother and father in an accident, Bandit takes
charge. Includes facts about the physical characteristics, behavior, habitat, and predators of the weasels.
    ISBN: 1-56763-785-X (hc)
            1-56763-786-8 (pbk)
    1. Weasels—Juvenile fiction. [1. Weasels—Fiction.]
I. Sargent, Pat, 1936- II. Huff, Jeane Lirley, 1946- ill.
III. Title. IV. Series: Sargent, Dave, 1941- Animal
pride series ; 14.

    PZ10.3.S243Ban 2003
    [Fic]—dc21   96-004618

Factual information excerpted/adapted from
THE WORLD BOOK ENCYCLOPEDIA.
© World Book, Inc. By permission of the publisher.
www.worldbook.com

Printed in the United States of America

Inspired by

the young weasels who lived on our farm. They were always stealing our eggs.

Dedicated to

our granddaughter Amber, who takes gum from her grandmother's purse when she is not watching.

Foreword

A young weasel family loses its mother and father. The young weasels have to learn to provide for themselves before they are really old enough. Bandit makes sure his little brothers and sisters have food.

Contents

If you would like to have the authors of the Animal Pride Series visit your school, free of charge, call 1-800-321-5671 or 1-800-960-3876.

One

No Mama

A family of weasels lived in an old rock fence on the north end of Farmer John's place. There were the mama, the daddy, and six little ones. The young weasels were about four weeks old, and they all looked alike. That is, all but one. He had black rings around his eyes. He looked like he was wearing a mask, so his mama named him Bandit.

Bandit was just starting to learn to fend for himself. Mama Weasel began taking Bandit and his brothers and sisters out to show them how to catch mice. Mama noticed that Bandit was a quick learner and she figured he would be able to provide for himself quite well when the time came for him to leave home.

Bandit was not only a good hunter, he was also very loving and caring. He helped his brothers and sisters to become better hunters by showing them some of the little tricks which came naturally to him.

When the young weasels were about ten weeks old, their mama and daddy were showing them how to catch ground squirrels. The squirrels had a den under some overhanging rocks. When they pulled the rocks away with their paws, the rocks fell, crushing Mama and Daddy Weasel. The six little weasels were all alone.

None of the six young weasels could catch any food to speak of, except Bandit. He led his brothers and sisters to a nearby field where there were lots of grasshoppers and crickets. Weasels like insects and bugs, even though it's not really their favorite meal. But crickets and grasshoppers as well as other insects are plentiful during the summer.

Bandit was catching the big ole grasshoppers right and left. When he got full, he watched the others as they tried to catch some. Not one of them could catch a grasshopper.

Bandit said, "Wait a minute! Don't you see what you're doing? You're scaring them away. Watch me closely and I'll show you how." The little weasels were hungry and knew they had better pay attention.

Bandit spotted a grasshopper just ahead. It was big! He pointed and whispered, "You see that one?" When they all nodded, Bandit said, "Watch me." He walked toward the big grasshopper. When he got close, he stopped. He waited for a couple of seconds, then pounced, landing smack on top of it.

Bandit gave the big grasshopper to Susie, who was the smallest, then told the others to try it again. They started chasing grasshoppers, but they still weren't having much luck.

Farmer John was out checking on the cows when he saw the young weasels chasing grasshoppers. At first, he thought they were playing, but after watching for a while, he knew they were hungry and were trying to catch grasshoppers to eat. Farmer John also noticed there was no mama and daddy weasel around. He knew they were orphans and he wasn't sure if they could survive.

Barney the Bear Killer always went with Farmer John to check the cows. Farmer John looked down and said, "Barney, don't bother those little weasels. I'm gonna leave some eggs in the chicken house today. If they find them, they can eat a few. But don't let anything in the chicken house except those young weasels!" Barney the Bear Killer wagged his tail, acknowledging the command.

They went back to the house, and Barney took up a position close to the chicken house. And sure enough, later that evening the young weasels smelled the eggs and came running. They had never eaten eggs before, but they knew that the eggs sure did smell good.

Two

Farmer John

Just as the young weasels got to the opening in the chicken house door, a white skunk came trotting up, hollering, "Get away from there! Those eggs are mine."

The weasels scurried around, trying to hide in the tall grass nearby. Just as the white skunk started to enter the chicken house, Barney let out a howl. The hair on the skunk's back stood straight up. It recognized that howl and knew from the sound that Barney the Bear Killer was near.

He whirled and ran for the woods with Ole Barney right behind him.

The young weasels lay silently in the tall grass for a long time. They could hear the faint sounds of Barney baying, which meant he was now a long way off.

Bandit was the first to come out of the tall grass. He started calling to the others, and one by one, they carefully joined Bandit near the opening of the chicken house.

Bandit crawled through the opening with his brothers and sisters close behind. Farmer John had laid a couple of eggs on the floor so the weasels could find them easily.

Bandit picked up one of the eggs with his front paws, but he couldn't find a way to open it. After a few minutes of rolling the egg around, he stood the egg up on one end and pecked on it with his teeth.

The soft shell cracked, making a small hole about the size of a pea. Bandit picked up the egg, turned the end with the hole to his mouth and sucked all the goodies out.

Bandit licked his lips, then rubbed his belly and told the others, "That was the best thing I have ever put in my mouth!"

The others had been watching Bandit to make sure the eggs were good to eat before they tried one. So now that they knew the eggs were good, they all scurried up the walls to get to the nest where there were more eggs. Bandit ate the other egg that lay on the floor.

By the time Bandit finished the egg and crawled to the chicken nest, the rest of the eggs were gone. It didn't take long for the weasels to eat the eggs that Farmer John had left for them.

The young weasels crawled out of the chicken house and headed down the hill toward the woods.

When they came to a fence, Bandit stopped and looked around. The others didn't know what he was doing, so they just stopped and watched him. After a few moments, Bandit looked at the others and said, "You know, we should dig a burrow here by the fence instead of going to our home down by the river. There is plenty of food here, so we won't have to travel far. The chicken house is just up the hill, and just look at all the grasshoppers right here at our front door."

One of Bandit's sisters asked, "But where will we get our water, Bandit? I'm thirsty now."

Bandit thought for a minute, then answered, "We'll look around and see if we can find water nearby. If we can't, we will have to make a trip to the river every day to get a drink. I think this would be a much better place for us to live."

Bandit told the others to start digging a burrow, and he would go look for water. All of them wanted to go with Bandit. They had now accepted him as their leader, and they didn't want to be away from him for even a minute.

Bandit said, "All right. Line up and follow me." They headed out across the field in search of water.

The young weasels traveled for only a short way when they came to a small hill. Bandit looked back at the others and said, "Let's climb to the top of this hill and see if we can see any water." All the weasels scampered to the top of the hill and looked around.

Susie hollered, "Look, Bandit," pointing to the field just ahead. "Isn't that water?" she asked.

"It sure looks like it," Bandit replied.

All the weasels hurried down the small hill and headed for the pond, which lay just ahead. They all got a badly needed drink of water.

The young weasels headed back to start digging their new burrow. They took turns digging through the night, and by first light of morning, they had a nice burrow tunneled out. They even dug a second entrance to the tunnel. Finally, the little weasels settled into their new home for a long well-deserved sleep.

Three

Growing Up

It was late afternoon when the weasels woke up. Susie was the first to awaken. She poked Bandit and said, "I'm thirsty, Bandit."

Bandit woke the others. There was lots of yawning and stretching going on for three or four minutes. Once they were all awake, they headed for the pond to get a drink.

On the way to the pond, they saw the small hill they had climbed the day before when they were out searching for water. There was a young blonde-headed girl on top of the hill, petting a little red fox. The little fox took off, running around and around the hill. The little girl was right behind it, chasing it.

The weasels didn't know what to think about all of this, so they lay on the grass and watched for a while. They were very amused. First the girl chased the fox, and then the fox chased the girl. This went on for a long time. They finally stopped, and the little girl skipped across the field toward Farmer John's house. The fox sat on top of the small hill and watched her. It finally ran down the hill and into its den just a short way from the top of the hill. The weasels got up and continued their journey to the pond for a drink of water.

After tanking up on water, Bandit, who had taken up a position on top of the pond bank, reared up on his back legs and said, "Let's go check out the chicken house and see if there are any eggs in it."

Without hesitation, the young weasels scampered straight toward the chicken house. They were not in single file now. Each was trying to outrun the other. Bandit had helped them to overcome their fears, and today they were feeling good.

When they reached the chicken house, the weasels climbed to the nest. There were only six eggs—one for each of them.

After eating the eggs, the little weasels headed for the tall grass just up the hill from their burrow and started catching big grasshoppers. Once they were full, they returned to their burrow and began digging.

They dug two more tunnels that led to their bedroom. This would give them lots of room to play and, if an enemy tried to enter their home, they would be able to escape using one of the other tunnels.

At sunup, the weasels went to bed and slept until nearly sundown. When they woke up, they made their regular rounds.

Over the next few days, the

young weasel family lived the life of total relaxation. They wanted for nothing. Then, one evening when they went to the chicken house for their supper, they got a big surprise. There were no eggs in the nest. They were tired of grasshoppers, so they went to the tall grass and began hunting for mice.

During the next few days, the weasels became very good hunters. They continued to visit the chicken house every day, but they found eggs only once every three or four days.

Farmer John had left the eggs in the chicken house to help the young weasels survive. But he also knew as they got older that he would have to force them to make do for themselves. That's why he had left eggs in the chicken house only once every three or four days.

The weasels now went farther from the burrow alone. At first, they went only a short distance. But as time passed, they went farther and farther away.

One day, they went on their last hunting trip as a family, for when they neared the chicken house, they saw Barney the Bear Killer lying in wait in front of the door. When they got close, he let out a bay and chased them away.

After that, the weasels decided it was best to hunt alone. It would be much easier for one weasel to escape Barney. They knew that he'd be waiting for them every night.

The young weasels were now six months old and capable hunters. They only saw each other during the day when they were sleeping. They would stay together as a family until spring. They would be a year old then.

When the robins arrived and new green blades of grass started peeking through the dead brown stubble from the year before, the weasels knew it was spring. They left the burrow they had dug together to Bandit. This was their way of showing their appreciation for all he had done for them.

When the weasels left, they knew they would see each other from time to time, but they vowed they would never forget the good times they'd had together.

Four

Weasel Facts

Weasels are small furry animals that have long slender bodies and short legs. They have very alert black or dark brown eyes and small rounded ears.

Weasels are found on every continent except Australia, Africa, and Antarctica.

The long-tailed weasel grows to be twelve to eighteen inches long, and weighs up to nine ounces. The females are smaller and weigh three to four ounces.

The ermine is a type of small weasel. Male ermines grow to be nine to thirteen inches long.

The smallest weasel is the smallest flesh-eating animal in the world. It grows up to ten inches long and weighs about two ounces.

Most weasels have brownish, reddish brown, or yellowish brown fur on their backs and sides, and white, yellowish, or tan fur on the underparts. In winter, the fur of weascls that live in cold climates changes to white, except for a black-tipped tail. The white fur provides camouflage in the snow. The black-tipped tail may catch the eye of an attacking predator, such as a hawk or owl, and cause the attacker to miss the weasel.

Weasels found in Florida and the southwestern United States sometimes have distinctive whitish or buff markings on the face.

Weasels have keen smell and vision. They are amazingly strong for their size and prey on mice and squirrels. They usually bite their victims on the neck or at the base of the skull. Weasels also eat insects, earthworms, frogs, lizards, rabbits, shrews, snakes, and birds. The weasel's slender body enables it to easily invade mouse burrows, rock crevices, and squirrel burrows.

Weasels often raid chicken yards and kill more chickens than they need for food. As a result, many farmers dislike weasels even though they destroy farmyard pests. The weasel's chief enemies are great horned owls and people. Weasels, like skunks, discharge a foul-smelling liquid called musk when they are threatened or attacked.

Weasels live in a variety of environments. They make dens in rock piles, under tree stumps, and in abandoned rodent burrows. They sometimes catch food in their dens and make nests using the fur and feathers of their victims. Weasels are most active at night.

Most females give birth to four to eight young at a time.

BEYOND "THE END"

LANGUAGE LINKS

Weasels are generally characterized by long and slender bodies with long necks, flat narrow heads with very alert black or dark brown eyes and small rounded ears, short limbs, and medium to long tails. The weasel's feet have five fingers with sharp claws. The color of weasels is chocolate brown on their backsides and white with brown spots on the underparts.

Now it is your turn to describe your characteristics. Swap with a friend to trace your body shape on a large piece of art paper. On this shape, write a description of your body using the weasel description above as a guide. Be sure to use plenty of adjectives (words that describe)! Do not sign your name. Display the "Class Characters" and let everyone read the descriptions and guess who they are.

CURRICULUM CONNECTIONS

When weasels are first born, they are dependent on their parents for food and shelter. So are you. As they grow, kits learn to hunt and care for themselves. So do you. Kits will grow up to be weasels and children will grow up to be adults. Talk about self-help skills students have learned at different ages and what they will learn when they are older. Draw a time line to show skills they have learned and will learn in the future. Include things such as feeding and dressing themselves, putting away toys, making the bed, doing dishes, using the telephone, staying home alone, driving a car, and getting a job.

After Bandit discovered the secret of making a small hole in the end of an egg and sucked all the goodies out, he licked his lips and told the others, "That was the best thing I have ever put in my mouth!" We, too, have learned how good eggs are. But when we are first asked to crack and separate the yolk of an egg from the white, we are as lost as Bandit! Go to web site <www.learn2.com/05/0573/05736.asp> to learn how to separate an egg and how to boil an egg!

Did you know you could tell a raw egg from a boiled egg by spinning it? A raw egg will wobble; a hard-boiled egg will spin easily!

THE ARTS

You have sung the nursery rhyme, *Pop Goes The Weasel*, many times. Now you can paint the rhyme online! There are other rhymes you can paint also. Go to web site <www.enchantedlearning.com/paint/rhymes/coloring> and follow the directions. What fun!

THE BEST I CAN BE

Think about all the manners your parents are teaching you, to say please and thank you, to be polite and respectful, to be responsible and accept consequences for your actions, and to help one another. Do you think these skills are as important to pave the way to a good and happy life for you as the life-skills discussed earlier? Why?